1935 if read a good book, either a lot of money or a library card. Cheap paperbacks were available, but their poor production generally mirrored the quality between the covers. One weekend that year, Allen Lane, Managing Director of The Bodley Head, having spent the weekend visiting Agatha Christie, found himself on a platform at Exeter station trying to find something to read for his journey back to London. He was appalled by the quality of the material he had to choose from. Everything that Allen Lane achieved from that day until his death in 1970 was based on a passionate belief in the existence of 'a vast reading public for *intelligent* books at a low price'. The result of his momentous vision was the birth not only of Penguin, but of the 'paperback revolution'. Quality writing became available for the price of a packet of cigarettes, literature became a mass medium for the first time, a nation of book-borrowers became a nation of book-buyers – and the very concept of book publishing was changed for ever. Those founding principles – of quality and value, with an overarching belief in the fundamental importance of reading – have guided everything the company has done since 1935. Sir Allen Lane's pioneering spirit is still very much alive at Penguin in 2005. Here's to the next 70 years!

MORE THAN A BUSINESS

'We decided it was time to end the almost customary half-hearted manner in which cheap editions were produced – as though the only people who could possibly want cheap editions must belong to a lower order of intelligence. We, however, believed in the existence in this country of a vast reading public for intelligent books at a low price, and staked everything on it'
Sir Allen Lane, 1902–1970

'The Penguin Books are splendid value for sixpence, so splendid that if other publishers had any sense they would combine against them and suppress them'
George Orwell

'More than a business ... a national cultural asset'
Guardian

'When you look at the whole Penguin achievement you know that it constitutes, in action, one of the more democratic successes of our recent social history'
Richard Hoggart

9th & 13th

JONATHAN COE

PENGUIN BOOKS

PENGUIN BOOKS

Published by the Penguin Group
Penguin Books Ltd, 80 Strand, London WC2R 0RL, England
Penguin Group (USA) Inc., 375 Hudson Street, New York, New York 10014, USA
Penguin Group (Canada), 10 Alcorn Avenue, Toronto, Ontario, Canada M4V 3B2
(a division of Pearson Penguin Canada Inc.)
Penguin Ireland, 25 St Stephen's Green, Dublin 2, Ireland
(a division of Penguin Books Ltd)
Penguin Group (Australia), 250 Camberwell Road, Camberwell, Victoria 3124,
Australia (a division of Pearson Australia Group Pty Ltd)
Penguin Books India Pvt Ltd, 11 Community Centre,
Panchsheel Park, New Delhi – 110 017, India
Penguin Group (NZ), cnr Airborne and Rosedale Roads, Albany,
Auckland 1310, New Zealand (a division of Pearson New Zealand Ltd)
Penguin Books (South Africa) (Pty) Ltd, 24 Sturdee Avenue,
Rosebank 2196, South Africa

Penguin Books Ltd, Registered Offices: 80 Strand, London WC2R 0RL, England

www.penguin.com

This collection published as a Pocket Penguin 2005
2

Copyright © Jonathan Coe, 1995, 1997, 1998, 2005
All rights reserved

'Ivy and Her Nonsense' previously appeared in *The Penguin Collection* (1995), '9th &
13th' in *The Time Out Book of New York Short Stories* (1997) and 'V.O.' in *New Writing 7*
(1998). '9th & 13th' also exists in a recorded version, with piano accompaniment written and performed by Danny Manners, on a CD of the same name released in
France on the Tricatel label (Tricatel album 18), which can (sporadically) be obtained
from the website *www.tricatel.com*. 'Diary of an Obsession' has never appeared in
English before, having been commissioned by *Cahiers du cinéma*.

The moral right of the author has been asserted

Set in 10.5/12pt Monotype Dante
Typeset by Palimpsest Book Production Limited
Polmont, Stirlingshire
Printed in England by Clays Ltd, St Ives plc

Contents

Introduction 1

Ivy and Her Nonsense 3

9th & 13th 20

V.O. 29

Diary of an Obsession 44

I.M.
James Eastwood Kay
1902–1985

Introduction

This collection represents my complete output of short stories in the last fifteen years, which is a bit of a joke. I thought of calling it *The Collected Shorter Prose*, but decided that the joke might then become laboured. I don't find it easy to write over a short distance, being drawn to complexity and panorama in fiction. Ideas which begin as short stories (such as *The House of Sleep*) usually turn into novels after a while. Three times, however, in response to pressure from friendly editors or publishers, I have managed to exercise some restraint on myself, and the results are printed here. 'Ivy and Her Nonsense' previously appeared in *The Penguin Collection* (1995), '9th & 13th' in *The Time Out Book of New York Short Stories* (1997) and a longer, less wieldy version of 'V.O.' in *New Writing 7* (1998). '9th & 13th' also exists in spoken form, with piano accompaniment written and performed by Danny Manners, on a CD of the same name released in France on the Tricatel label (Tricatel album 18). It is still sporadically available online, at *www.tricatel.com*.

For seven or eight years at the start of my career I wrote criticism fairly regularly for the newspapers, and my first thought on being asked to compile this short book was that it provided a perfect moment to rescue some lost journalistic gems from undeserved obscurity. Having trawled through my hard disk, however, I've reached the conclusion that obscurity is exactly what most of that writing does deserve. I've made an exception for one piece only, 'Diary of an Obsession', which has never appeared in

English before, having been commissioned by *Cahiers du cinéma*. I like this piece because it puts on record my admiration for Billy Wilder and one of his greatest though most misunderstood films; and because it also concerns, in part, my grandfather James Kay – a figure who also materializes, fictionalized, in 'Ivy and Her Nonsense'. My grandfather died more than twenty years ago, but I still dream about him often, and talk about him to my own daughters. His dynamism, his dry sense of humour and his love of reading were all vital influences on my childhood. Almost the last advice he gave to me before dying was to become a teacher and to 'forget about writing for a long, long time'. Like all his advice, it was offered with love, and with my best interests at heart. I would have liked him to see my work get published, although his own verdicts on my books would have been severe. It seems right, somehow, that this little volume should be dedicated to him.

Ivy and Her Nonsense

When I came out of the church and crunched back down the gravel path towards the plot where my grandparents were buried, I found that Gill was still standing by their gravestone, staring across the churchyard with a strange, frozen look in her eye.

It was a grey and breezy morning, two days before Good Friday. The wind, blowing in wild, unpredictable gusts, carried the noise of traffic from the distant M54, and had already tipped our freshly laid wreath to one side. I knelt and straightened it.

'What now?' I said. 'Home?'

She didn't answer. She turned towards me with a frown, and seemed on the point of asking a question when a noise behind us caused her to look round sharply. It was the wicket gate to the churchyard, blowing open and shut in the wind.

'Has there been anyone else here?' she asked. 'Besides us, I mean. Have you seen anyone?'

I shook my head. We had arrived in the village only half an hour ago, and had found it empty and somnolent. My sister now hugged her coat tightly around herself and began making her way slowly back to the car; her gaze fixed on the ground, her boots tracing patterns in the gravel as she walked. But then before reaching the porch she suddenly turned again. She stared hard at a chestnut tree which stood against the furthest wall, over towards the bowling green. Beneath it was a wooden bench.

'Anything the matter?' I asked.

'I'll tell you later.'

I offered to drive, and asked her if she was still in the mood for the sentimental journey we'd proposed on the way over from Birmingham. She gave an absent nod, and so I reversed out into the main thoroughfare, paused uncertainly at the first junction, and then struck off down a once-familiar lane, verdant this morning and windswept. After a few minutes, during which the windscreen became spattered with thin raindrops, my grandparents' house came into view. We parked on the grass verge about fifty yards from the front gate, and looked at it blankly, not knowing what to do next.

'They've changed the whole shape of it, haven't they?'

The new owners – as I still thought of them, fifteen years after they'd moved in – had added a two-storey extension where my grandfather had once built his long, lean-to workshop along one side of the house.

'I suppose it's quite tasteful, actually,' I conceded. 'Credit where it's due.'

I looked across at Gill, expecting her to have some thoughts on the matter. But her eyes were closed, and one hand was resting against her temple, as if she had a headache. I took hold of her other hand and found it ice-cold.

She said: 'I'm sorry. Something strange happened back there, that's all.' Then she blew her nose into a Kleenex (she kept a copious supply tucked up both arms of her cardigan) and added: 'Let's go, shall we? I don't think I can face the farmhouse.'

So: did she really see a ghost in the churchyard that morning – or two ghosts, to be more precise? She has always stood by her story, and it has only ever been pride, I suppose, that has stopped me from fully believing her: the sense of some subtle family insult – the sense, if you will, of having been 'cut' – upon learning that it was Gill my grandparents had chosen to appear before, rather than myself. Certainly she was able to describe the scene in convincing detail. My grandfather had been sitting on the bench with his briar-wood pipe in his mouth (unlit), his hearing aid in place, and wearing his thick woollen herringbone overcoat; my grand-mother had been carrying, as usual, the thermos flask she had bought at Woolworth's countless decades ago, which had accompanied us on all our childhood picnics and excur-sions. They had seemed relaxed, Gill said, and contented – although clearly feeling the cold – and they had also been entirely self-absorbed; occupied in a voluble and animated conversation (an odd feature, this, which did not chime with my own memories of their relationship), and oblivious to the watchful presence of my sister. The illusion, if that's what it was, had lasted about ten or fifteen seconds.

Gill told me this as we drove home, following the faster, recently completed roads which did indeed knock a few minutes off the old journey, although only because they bypassed all the towns, villages and landmarks which had once made it interesting. As she spoke about her peculiar visitation, I was still acutely conscious of being treated as her little brother, and could detect in her manner an undertone of childlike competitiveness. It was as if she knew that by describing it so completely, and in such matter-of-fact terms, she could retrospectively devalue my own limited experience in this area. It was only a matter of time before I rose to the bait; and so when at last she said to me, flatly, 'I can see you don't believe a word of this', I heard myself replying:

'Of course I do. Of course. Don't forget that something similar happened to me once, after all.'

She smiled, and her eyes gleamed with satisfaction. 'Oh, come on – you're not going to bring out *that* old story again, are you?'

'It happened. I didn't imagine it.'

'But you were tiny. We were both just little kids. *And* you were half asleep at the time.'

I dropped the subject, having no serious desire to submit my memories to her mischievous scrutiny yet again. But after lunch, as I drove, alone, back up the hill to my parents' house, I felt myself once more surrendering to recollection. I remembered the weekly visits we used to pay to Shropshire as children; the summer holidays, with their morning fishing trips and long afternoons sitting alone in the dining room, reading books and listening to the slow tick of the grandfather clock. I remembered the Christmas mornings, opening presents after breakfast and then being dragged out on walks across frost-hardened fields beneath a clear winter sky. And one Christmas I remembered above all.

That afternoon, when I took a ladder and climbed up to my parents' loft, I wasn't entirely sure what I was looking for, but allowed myself to be drawn towards a pile of cardboard boxes stacked beneath the eaves in the furthest and most shadowy corner. My torchlight picked out this jumble of rubbish and rested on it, bringing it into brilliant relief: my childhood. I approached it warily, crouching, avoiding the low beams, and then sat apprehensive for a few moments before brushing the dust off the first box and peering inside.

There was no time to do more than glance at the damp and wrinkled pages of old notepads and diaries, or to flick through the ancient scrapbooks into which I had once pasted, with manic diligence, hundreds of cuttings about my favourite footballers and pop stars. Before long I had come upon a small wooden box filled with Kodak slides, and this I seized eagerly, taking them out and holding them up to the torchlight one by one. Forgotten holidays, forgotten gardens, forgotten family cars, forgotten relatives. There I was on the beach at Llanbedrog with Aunt Ivy and Uncle Owen: I looked four or five years old and, unconscious of the camera, was caught in a relaxed pose, one hand stuck blissfully down the front of my swimming trunks. My great aunt and uncle sat on their beach towels and smiled the trusting, confident smiles of people who had survived a war, prospered in the years that followed, and were not yet touched by the new uncertainties of the 1960s. I could hear their voices again – his a deep and guttural drone; hers shrill and deliberate – mixed with the cries of children and the slow wash of water against the shingle. My past was full of voices: the continuous soundtrack of my family as they talked, gossiped, bickered. How quiet the village had seemed today, by comparison. I was glad we hadn't driven up to Uncle Owen's old farmhouse, now empty and shuttered.

But here *was* the farmhouse, on the very next slide. The whole family was sitting down to supper in the kitchen – apart from my father, who must have been taking the picture. There were eleven of us, in all, and we were raising our glasses, and smiling, and wearing Christmas party hats: mine was too big for me, and had slipped down over one eye. Only my grandmother, I noticed, scrutinizing the image more closely, seemed to be set apart from the general hilarity. She looked detached and pensive, leading me to believe that this was the very same Christmas I had been thinking of – the one just after her spell of jury service. For a while I stared wonderingly at this miniature tableau, which seemed to contain a world every bit as mysterious and implausible as an impossibly scratchy old film. And I was still staring, still trying to fathom its secret, when my torch – its battery clearly on its last legs – began to flicker, fade and at last gave out, plunging me all at once into the inky blackness of memory.

In those days we used to travel to Shropshire every year to spend Christmas at my grandparents' house. We would arrive late in the afternoon on Christmas Eve, and after a brief, energetic bout of unpacking, the grown-ups would sit down to drink sherry and exchange bits of news. The sitting room would be even brighter and more cheerful than usual: its long windows looked out over both the front and back gardens, and the last of the sunlight, sharpened by snow, would catch the baubles and trinkets hanging from my grandfather's tree, winking back at us from the tinsel draped over its thick branches.

'Well, Ma, you seem to have survived your ordeal,' said my mother this time, as Gill and I helped ourselves from a plate of digestive biscuits and tried not to look restless.

'Oh, it wasn't too bad. I'm just glad it was over in time for Christmas. I haven't got half the things done.' She glanced severely at my grandfather. 'Of course, Jim hasn't been much help.'

He ignored the rebuke, choosing instead to mutter: 'Pity you didn't come to the right decision.'

'Oh, Dad, don't you start,' said my mother, and then Gill managed to change the subject by asking if it was time to feed the horses yet.

My grandparents owned a few acres of land adjoining the house, and here they looked after two racehorses belonging to their neighbours, who kept an extensive stable. It was a favourite ritual to accompany my grandfather, still broad and muscular in his old age, as he carried bales of hay down to the paddock where the horses would be standing in patient anticipation, flank to flank. I felt sorry for them today, for the cold made my hands ache, even with gloves on. We ran on ahead, armed with sugar lumps to give them a treat.

'What was Grandma's ordeal?' I asked Gill, who was, in my experience, a fount of knowledge.

'You don't know anything, do you?' she said: which was

true. 'She's been to court. A woman killed her husband, and she had to decide whether she was guilty or not. She was in the jury. Mum said it was in all the papers, but she wouldn't let me see them.'

My grandfather had nearly caught us up, so she sank to a whisper: 'She did it with a knife. First of all he was going to stab her, but then she got hold of the knife and stabbed him: hundreds and hundreds of times. With a penknife – just like I'm going to get for Christmas.'

This explanation, although graphic, was far from satisfactory, but I had the edge over my elder sister in one respect: I knew where my grandparents kept the old newspapers – they were stacked up in Grandpa's workshop, awaiting the next bonfire. I slipped in there before tea and spent a damp and chilly few minutes leafing through the pages of the *Shropshire Star*. The familiar smells of turps and wood shavings were tempered, today, by the sweet scent of satsumas: doubtless they were in their usual hiding place, but I was too preoccupied to filch one. As it turned out, I didn't have far to look for my story: it was there on the front page of one of the most recent editions. 'KNIFE WOMAN GETS FIVE YEARS' was the headline in enormous letters, and underneath, slightly smaller, it said: 'Jury finds her not guilty of murder.'

As I read the report, numerous fragments of adult conversation which had fallen my way over the last few months began at last to make sense. This was a case which had divided the local community, and indeed my family: for the couple in question had lived only a few miles away, and such sensational events were rare in this placid part of the world. The wife had been unfaithful to the husband; he had threatened to kill her, on several occasions; and one night, when he had finally seemed on the point of carrying out his threat, she had forestalled him by snatching the penknife from his hand and plunging it repeatedly into his chest. My family's interest had risen to a pitch when my grandmother was asked to serve on the jury which would hear the case, and I imagine that she found it a deeply troubling experience. A quiet, unassumingly religious woman, she must have felt lost in this world of ferocious passions, and things can't have been helped by strong hints from her more puritanical relatives – notably her sister – to the effect that the wife was nothing but a Jezebel and a harlot who deserved to be put away for life. In the end the jury had come to a different conclusion; and although the phrases they invoked – such as 'unsound mind' and 'mitigating circumstances' – carried only a hazy meaning for me, I found myself very much in agreement when I saw the newspaper photograph of the murdered husband. 'The face that will haunt her for ever,' it said, and I could see why. He looked much more like a killer than she did, and even in that smudged, grainy reproduction his sunken eyes – which seemed hollow and threatening at the same time – exerted a horrible fascination. They burned into me so powerfully, in fact, that when I heard the call for tea, out of some perverse and heedless impulse I quickly tore the picture out and carried it unseen up to our bedroom.

Supper on Christmas Eve was provided by my great aunt and uncle, round at their farmhouse, and it followed an obligatory game of charades which gave Gill further scope to demonstrate her ingenuity. For this purpose, the family gathered in the great drawing room, with its open fire and heavy, faded armchairs. Sending Gill out into the corridor, we would choose a television personality for her to identify, and she would return breathlessly eager to face our impersonations which never had her beaten for more than three guesses. Tommy Cooper presented no problems at all;

neither did Uncle Owen's failed attempt to defy gravity by raising his arms and legs together, like a pair of scissors.

'Harry Worth,' said Gill, blushing with pleasure.

For supper we had cold meat, pork pies, beetroot, celery and jacket potatoes rolled in salt and pepper. This was another time for adult talk, while Gill and I had to be content with kicking each other excitedly under the table. If we made enough noise about it we could pretend not to be listening to the general conversation, which might then become agreeably uninhibited.

'I should like to know,' said Aunt Ivy, addressing her sister in her usual strident monotone (she was by then almost completely deaf), 'why you decided to let that creature off scot-free.'

'Give over, woman,' said Uncle Owen. 'You don't know the facts. You only know what you read in the paper.'

My mother agreed. 'She said it was in self-defence: and if you saw the picture of her husband in the newspaper, you'd believe her.'

'It was a difficult choice,' said my grandmother. 'A very difficult choice. I never did make up my mind entirely, like some of the others. It seemed the Christian thing to do. People like that deserve pity. They've got God to answer to. All the same,' she dabbed her lips with a beetroot-stained napkin, 'he never did attack her, as such. He only threatened her.'

'Threatened her!' said Uncle Owen. 'I'll say he did. Threatened to cut her throat, didn't he?'

'Ssh!' said someone, while Gill, unobserved, performed a short pantomime for my benefit: she raised her bread-knife and drew it slowly across her throat, smiling like a little demon. For a moment I had to fight back tears.

Then crackers were pulled, and hats distributed, and photographs taken; and despite the fact that my hat was too big, and I didn't understand any of the riddles, and Gill got a compass while all I got was a whistle that didn't blow, my spirits rallied considerably.

After supper, while the others took their coffee into the drawing room, we stayed behind to feed scraps to the three spaniel puppies which had spent the last half-hour shut in a back parlour and scratching excitedly at the kitchen door. Partly to keep Gill off the subject of murder, I said something about her being good at charades, and asked if there was a secret to it: whereupon, much to my surprise, and with a pleased, confidential grin, she pulled a heavy key out of her pocket.

'Come with me,' she said, and led me into the hall, where a door beneath the oak staircase, normally kept locked, led down into the wine cellar. She explained that you could get right under the drawing room and hear every word that was said. 'Didn't you wonder why I was always out of breath?'

'Can we try it now?' I asked, very struck with the possibilities of this system.

'OK.' She unlocked the door. 'You first.'

Of course the first thing I heard was the door slamming behind me, and the turn of the key in the lock. I pounded on the panels and shouted a bit, but I knew that Gill would want to make me wait. I was determined to try her trick, anyway, so once I had found the light switch I took a deep breath and headed bravely down the stairs, leaving her to listen in vain for my entreaties.

The cellar actually contained more fruit than wine, and more spiders' webs than either. Further, less awestruck exploration in later years would reveal it to be quite compact, but that night it seemed labyrinthine and unending: there were different chambers leading off on both sides of a main passageway which itself took several unexpected turns, and I had to peep round each corner nervously before I dared move closer towards the voices which were becoming slowly more distinct above my head. Along the walls, where coarse brick showed beneath a thin layer of whitewash, I could see the silvery trails of slugs.

Once I was standing directly beneath the drawing room, the conversation would have been easy to hear even if the dominant voice had not been my Aunt Ivy's.

'Are you not even a little scared, though?' she was saying.

'Oh Ivy, will you stop mithering, for Heaven's sake.'

'You know I don't believe in any of that foolishness,' said my grandmother. 'The Christian religion is all I need to believe in, and I would have thought the same went for you, since I presume you'll be reading in church tonight.'

'Rather you than me, dear. That's all I'm saying.'

'Stop werreting, Ivy. A joke's a joke.'

('Werreting' was a favourite local word, more or less synonymous with 'mithering'. Nobody ever explained to me what 'mithering' meant.)

'Anyway,' Ivy persisted, 'you get ghosts in churches, too. That's a proven fact.'

'The Holy Ghost,' suggested Uncle Owen wittily.

'I'm talking about Chetwynd churchyard, outside Newport. Have you never seen the ghost of Madam Piggott, flitting about in her nightgown and combing her baby's hair amongst the graves?'

'Why, have you?'

'Not personally, no. But I've sat in that churchyard, with the leaves rustling about my head, and the trees bending and moaning, and not a breath of wind in the air.'

My great uncle, perhaps through daily contact with his pigs, had built up an expressive repertoire of grunts, and he now let out a particularly good one. I could hear the clink of Aunt Ivy's coffee cup as she laid it down for emphasis.

'All I'm saying is that this man, who was murdered by his wife in cold blood, is one man who'll not be resting quiet in his grave tonight. I know what I'd be doing if I was him. I'd be paying a visit on those people who'd passed up the chance to avenge me. That's what I'd do.'

And as I took in these words, only half comprehending, sudden fear caused me to turn. A huge human shadow was forming in the passageway, looming larger and larger, advancing towards me with a remorseless tread. Having nowhere to run, I could only shrink back into the wall, and feel my terror shade deliciously into relief as I saw Gill coming round the corner to tell me that my ordeal was over.

That Christmas, for the first time, it had been decided that we were old enough to attend midnight communion with the rest of the family. We drove to the village church in two cars: ever hungry for novelty, Gill and I had chosen to travel with our grandparents. We trembled with anticipation on the back seat, watching the headlamps throw patterns of light on the high, frosty hedgerows.

'Ivy and her nonsense,' said my grandmother, tutting. 'Heaven only knows why they allow her to read in church at all. Everybody knows she's the least religious person in the village.'

'You know perfectly well why they let her read,' said Grandpa. 'It's because her voice carries.'

I don't remember much about the service, my first experience of Anglican ritual. I know that I listened out for references to the Holy Ghost, but they didn't sound very frightening – not like the walk through the churchyard afterwards. It seemed a dismal and a lonely place, despite the voices I could hear all around me, chattering and calling out goodbyes and wishing each other seasonal compliments. Even my grandfather, whose strong leathery hand engulfed my own, paused at one point to gaze at the scattered headstones, and I felt a shudder run through his body. Perhaps it was the cold, or perhaps the foreknowledge that he too would be lying there, in years to come, his grave chilled by an easterly wind.

Sharing a bedroom with Gill could often seem like a hardship, but tonight I was glad of the company. As usual, she was in no mood for sleep. Last year she had attempted to stay awake all night, hoping to discover more about the interesting process whereby two stockings came to be deposited at the foot of our beds, filled with sugar-coated sweets and chocolate pennies which were meant to serve as an appetizer for the main attractions downstairs. But this year, it seemed, she just wanted to talk.

'This penknife's going to be brilliant,' she said. 'I'm going to be the only girl at school who's got one.'

Gill was being provocative, because she knew that I was all set to become wildly jealous of this gift; I had not had the enterprise to ask for anything so exciting, having written a note to Father Christmas suggesting a pair of football boots. (And I didn't even really want those, but had done it to please my father, who was anxious for me to manifest some sporting inclinations.)

'How do you know he's going to bring you what you want?' I asked.

'What do you mean, "he"?' said Gill. She paused, then started giggling in a discomforting, private way.

'What are you laughing at?'

'You,' she said. 'You're so funny.'

She laughed a little more, and then fell silent. I could hear her breathing grow more regular. Outside there was a breeze getting up and the branches of the apple tree were starting to scrape across our window.

'Do you believe in ghosts, Gill?'

'No,' she murmured.

'Aunt Ivy does.'

'She's a stupid old woman. That's what Dad says.'

'What about that dead man?' I ventured. 'He must be ever so cross with Grandma.'

'Dead men can't be cross,' said Gill. 'Go to sleep.'

But I couldn't go to sleep. The wind grew fiercer and the whole house seemed to be filled with strange creaks and bangings: to my fevered imagination they were the sounds of doors opening, and heavy footsteps ascending the stairs. I got up and drew back the curtains, but in the moonlight our room was no less sinister, a world of suggestive outlines and thick pools of darkness. I fought against a host of shocking images: Gill pretending to cut her throat at the dinner table; the giant silhouette advancing on me in the cellar; my grandfather shivering at the sight of the midnight churchyard. Above all, I remembered the photograph of the murdered man which I had so recklessly cut from the pages of the local paper, and I was tense with the expectation that he might emerge at any moment, penknife in hand, from the shadows.

In these circumstances I did what any resourceful seven-year-old would have done: namely, I decided to wake up my parents. I had noticed that requests for admission to their bed rarely met with much opposition, and this was clearly an urgent case, because I was in no state to pass the night alone. So I quickly got up, wrapped my dressing gown around me and padded out onto the landing.

There, I saw something which surprised me. Everything was in darkness, except for a shaft of unsteady light visible from beneath the door of my grandparents' room. I'd assumed that all my family had gone to bed long ago, but it seemed inconsiderate to rouse my mother and father if it turned out that my grandparents were still awake. I altered my course, then, in the direction of their room, and after pausing outside for a few seconds, during which I heard not a sound, I wordlessly pushed the door open.

The flickering light must have been coming from a candle, because it was almost blown out as soon as I opened the door, letting in a draught of cold air. What happened next happened very quickly. The side of the bed which faced the door was my grandmother's, and I could make out her sleeping form as she lay quite still on her back. Sitting on the bed beside her was a man. His face was hidden in shadow at first: all I could see was the glint of a knife blade in his upraised hand. He jerked around as soon as I came in, and for a sudden, stretched moment we were staring at one another. His sunken eyes burned into mine: they were hollow and threatening at one and the same time. Then I turned and fled, back towards my parents' room where I flung open the door and had soon managed to rouse the entire house. Even Gill came running to see what was going on. And so, cradled by my mother as she sat bleary-eyed on the edge of her bed, I explained that I had just seen a ghost trying to kill Grandma.

'A ghost?'

'A man. He was sitting on the bed, right next to her.'

My grandfather arrived, still in his pyjamas.

'What's up?' he said.

'He saw you,' my mother whispered.

My grandfather put a finger to his lips and shook his head at her. To me he said: 'Sounds as though you've been having a nasty dream.'

'It *wasn't* a dream. It was the man. The man from the newspaper.'

Sensing that any attempt to resolve this situation by rational argument was doomed to failure, my mother sent everyone back to their beds; but for the time being she allowed me to stay in her room, where, cocooned between my parents' bodies, I must finally have drifted into a half-sleep. I can dimly remember being lifted by my father some time later, and carried back to my own room. The close of the door as he left must have wakened me completely; and then I could see Gill's eyes sparkling in the dark.

'You are a chump,' she said.

'Why am I?'

'That was Grandpa you saw. He was wrapping our presents.'

As soon as I registered these words, a new and difficult question started to form.

'How do you mean?' I said, slowly.

And this was how it came about that Gill – very much, I'm sure, to her own inexpressible triumph and delight – found herself in a position to tell me the less than magical truth about where our Christmas presents had been coming from all these years.

'So the knife . . .' I began.

'It was my present, of course. I told you I was going to get one.' She yawned and burrowed further into her tangle of sheets and blankets. 'Goodnight, chump.'

Stung by this parting insult, I answered, 'Goodnight – idiot' by way of riposte, and lay awake for some time wondering whether Gill was really so clever after all. In the silence of that night I turned her explanation over again and again in my mind, and found it wanting.

Christmas Day dawned at last, revealing the countryside shrouded beneath a new layer of deep virgin snow. The ploughed fields at the foot of the garden sent out ripples of undulating white, and the air that morning was so clear that if you stood on the terrace wall and looked towards the Wrekin, you could easily make out the Needle's Eye. Sunlight flooded the sitting room as we opened our presents after breakfast. Everyone was in high spirits; the alarms of the night were forgotten.

For once it was Gill's turn to be disappointed. My football boots were a perfect fit, as indeed was the coat my parents had bought for her. There were toys, books and board games in abundance. But there was no penknife. Apparently they had decided that it wouldn't make a suitable present for a young girl.

Later Gill tracked me down to the pantry – stuffing my pockets with mince pies in preparation for our morning walk – and got me up against the wall.

'You told me there was a penknife,' she said. 'You *told* me.'

'There was,' I protested.

'You lied to me.'

'I didn't. There was a knife. But it wasn't Grandpa I saw. I told you that.'

She relaxed her grip and stood back, regarding me fiercely.

'You're mad, you are,' she said. 'You're completely bats.'

That was her theory, anyway. But as soon as we returned from the walk and I had a moment to myself, it felt like an act of perfect sanity to run upstairs, fetch the newspaper photograph from my drawer and throw it on to the sitting room fire. Watching his face burn, blacken and vanish, I made a prayer to my newly acquired God that he would never visit us again.

9th & 13th

I live on the corner of 9th and 13th, and I promise you, it's not a good place to be. It's not a place where you'd want to linger. It's the sort of place you pass through; the sort you move on from. Or at least, that's what it is for most people. For everybody but me.

I can't believe I've been living here for more than eighteen months now. I can't believe that every morning, for the last eighteen months, I've been woken up by the rolling of shutters at the Perky Pig Diner and BBQ just across from my apartment. Shortly after that happens, the noises will start downstairs: furniture being shifted, trucks driving in and out right underneath my bedroom, the throb of their revving engines so insistent that even when I try to block it out by putting on my headphones and turning the keyboard's volume up to Max, even then I can still feel it through my feet. I live above the business premises of the Watson Storage and Removal Company: which makes sense, in a way, because like I said, this is a transient place, a place for people on the move, a place for people who are getting ready to pack up and leave.

9th and 13th. Do you know what that sounds like? You can find out for yourself, if there's a piano anywhere nearby. Start with . . . start with a C, if you like. Way down on the keyboard, two octaves below middle C. Hold it down with your little finger, and now stretch your fingers, really stretch them, more than an octave, until your thumb is on a D. Now play the two notes, and listen to the interval. You've got your 9th. It's slightly rootless, already: those two bass notes that don't quite agree with one another. There's an audible sense of indecision. And now, with the thumb of your right hand, you play a B flat. This adds a kind of bluesy overtone, turns the ambiguous statement of those two notes into a question. It seems to ask: where are we heading? To which the next note – another D – adds nothing except emphasis. Now the question seems even more urgent, but when the F is introduced, it changes everything. All of a sudden the chord feels hopeful, aspiring. There's the hint of an upward movement, the sense that we might be about to arrive somewhere. And then, finally, we add the A, so that we have our 13th interval at last: and listen to how plangent it makes it sound, how wistful. This chord is aching to resolve, to settle on something: C major would be the most obvious place to go next, but it could be A minor, or F major seven, or . . . well, anything. It's so open. As open as a chord can get. Brimming with potential.

9th and 13th. The sound of possibility.

And how long is it since I played those chords, now? How long since *she* came into the bar and stood over the piano as I improvised, in the half-dark, after even the most hardened drinkers had finished up and gone home? I don't know. I lose track. All I remember is that for a few minutes we talked, swapped a few banalities, as my fingers wandered trance-like over the keyboard, tracing the usual patterns, the easy, familiar harmonies that I'm locked into, these days, like a series of bad habits. She was from Franklin, Indiana, she said, and had only pitched up in New York that afternoon. She said she'd given up her job in the local record store and had come to the city to write. To write books. And that's all I ever found out about her – not even her name, just that she was from Franklin and that she was going to write and that she had dark hair, pulled severely back from her face into a short ponytail, and tiny freckles on either side of her nose, and brown-green eyes that narrowed to a smile whenever I looked at her. Which wasn't very often, I have to say, hunched as I was over the keyboard, picking my way slowly through those well-worn chords, until my hands finally gave up; faltered, and came to rest; came to rest where they always did. The usual place.

9th and 13th.

At which point – at which precise point – she asked me a question.

'Listen,' she said. 'Is there anywhere . . . do you know of anywhere that I can stay tonight? I don't have anywhere to stay.'

The possibilities raised by that question, like the possibilities raised by that chord, hung in the air for as long as it took the notes to decay.

Infinite possibilities.

To take just one of them, for instance. Supposing I had resolved the chord. Supposing I had resolved it in the most obvious way, with a soft – soft but insistent – C major. Perhaps with an A natural in there somewhere, to make it just a little more eloquent. And suppose I had answered her question by saying: 'Well, it's getting pretty late, and there aren't that many places around here. There's always my couch.'

What would have happened?

Where would I be now?

This is what would have happened:

Her eyes would have narrowed again, at first, in that warm, shy, smiling way she had, and then she would have looked away, gathering her thoughts for a moment or two, before turning back to me, and saying:

'Would that be OK? I mean, that's really nice of you . . .'

And I would have said: 'No problem. It's just a couple of blocks from here.'

'I don't want to put you to any trouble,' she would have said. 'It'll only be for one night.'

But it wouldn't only have been for one night. We both would have known that, even then.

I would have closed the lid of the piano and said good-night to Andy at the bar, collecting my fee (a thin wad of dollar bills from the cash register), and then opening the door for her, warning her to mind her step on the narrow, dimly lit staircase that led up to the street. She would have had a bag with her, a black canvas hold-all, and I would have offered to carry it, slinging it over my shoulder as I followed her up the stairs, admiring the sway of her back and the shapeliness of the stockinged ankle I would have glimpsed between the bottom of her jeans and her neat brown shoes.

Once out in the street, she would have pulled her coat tightly around herself, and looked to me for guidance – only her eyes visible above the turned-up collar – and I would have taken her arm gently and led her off down West 4th Street, heading north towards 9th and 13th.

'Are you sure this is all right?' she would have asked. 'I hate to think I might be imposing.'

And I would have said: 'Not at all. It's good of you to trust me, really. I mean, a total stranger . . .'

'Oh, but I'd been listening to you play the piano.' She would have glanced at me, now. 'I'd been in there for a couple of hours, and . . . Well, anyone who plays the piano like that must be a good person.' Then a nervous laugh, before offering up the compliment. 'You play very nicely.'

I would have smiled at that: a practised, rueful smile. 'You should tell that to the guy who runs the bar. He might pay me a little more.' After which, almost immediately, I would have been anxious to change the subject. 'My name's David, by the way.'

'Oh. I'm Rachel.' We would have shaken hands, a little awkwardly, a little embarrassed at our own formality, and then hurried on to my apartment, because Rachel would have been looking cold, already: her breath steaming in the frosty air, the hint of a chatter in her teeth.

'You probably want to get straight to bed,' I would have said, as soon as we got inside, and I would have helped her off with her coat and hung it up in the hall-way. I would have showed her where the bed was, and changed the sheets for her while she was in the bathroom. The old sheets and blankets I would have taken with me, using them to make up some sort of bed for myself on the couch. When she had finished in the bathroom I would have gone to check that she had every-thing she wanted, and then I would have said goodnight, but afterwards I would have lain on the couch for ten minutes or more, waiting for the light in her bedroom to be turned off. But she wouldn't have turned it off. Instead, her bedroom door would have been pulled slowly open, and I would have felt her looking at me, trying to work out if I had gone to sleep, before she tiptoed through into the hallway, and started searching through the pockets of her coat. A few seconds later she would have found what she was looking for and would have come back; and just as she was returning to the bedroom I would have said:

'Is everything OK?'

She would have started, and paused, before saying: 'Yes, I'm fine. I hope I didn't wake you.' And then: 'I forgot my notebook. I always try to write something in it, every night, before I go to bed. Wherever I am.'

'That's very disciplined of you,' I would have said. And she would have asked me:

'Don't you practise every night? Surely you must practise.'

'In the mornings, sometimes. By the time it gets this late, I'm too tired.'

She could have turned, and gone, at this point. The silence would have been long enough to allow it. But that wouldn't have happened. I would have sensed that she wanted to stay, and would have said:

'So what are you going to write now?'

'Just a few . . . thoughts, you know. Just a few thoughts about the day.'

'You mean like a diary?'

'I suppose.'

'I've never done anything like that. Never kept a diary. Have you always kept one?'

'Yes. Since I was a child. I remember, when I was about seven, or eight . . .' We would have talked, then, for fifteen minutes or more. Or rather, I would have listened (because that's always how it is) while she talked; talked, and came closer – sitting on the arm of the couch, at first, then sitting beside me, after I had shifted over to make room for her, her bare thighs (because she would have been wearing only a T-shirt and panties) in contact with my hips: only the sheets and blankets intervening.

I know, too, what would have happened at the end of those fifteen minutes. How she would have leaned towards me, leaned over me, the heaviness of her body against mine. How her hair, freed now from its ponytail, would have drifted across my face until she brushed it back, and how her lips would have touched mine: her lips dry with the cold. Dry at first. How I would have followed her into

25

the bedroom. How there would have been a rapid, almost imperceptible shedding of our last remaining clothes. How I would have learned about her by touch, first of all, and by sight only later, when the bedclothes lay dishevelled, thrust aside, strewn across the floor. How willingly she would have given herself to me. And how beautiful she would have been, by the flashes of neon through the uncurtained window. How very beautiful.

How right for me.

That's what would have happened. And this is what would have happened next.

In the morning, we would have had breakfast together at the Perky Pig, and even that would have tasted good, for once. Over refills of coffee, we would have made plans. First of all, there would have been the question of accommodation: it would have been blindingly obvious that we could afford a bigger and better place if we pooled our resources and moved in together. But that would have presented another problem: her parents, both Christian fundamentalists, would never have countenanced this arrangement. We would have to get married. The suggestion would have been made jokingly, at first, but it would only have taken a few seconds for our eyes to make contact and to shine with the sudden, instantaneous knowledge that it was what we both wanted. Three days later, man and wife, we would have spotted an advertisement in the *New York Review of Books* for a vacant apartment in the West Village, offered at a derisory rent to suitably Bohemian tenants. It would have been the property of a middle-aged academic couple, about to depart for a five-year sojourn in Europe. Arranged over three floors, it would have included an enormous studio room – at the centre of which would have stood a Steinway baby grand, sheened in winter sunshine from the skylight – and a small but adorable garret study with a view over the treetops of Washington Square. In this study, during the next few weeks, Rachel would have written the final chapters of her almost-completed novel. A novel which, after two regretful but encouraging rejections, would have been accepted for publication by Alfred A. Knopf, and would have appeared the following September, becoming the sensation of that fall. Meanwhile, as her book climbed the bestseller lists and scooped up prizes, I would have finished my long-projected piano concerto, an early performance of which (at the Merkin Concert Hall, with myself both playing and conducting) would have caught the attention of Daniel Barenboim, who would have insisted on programming it as the chief item in his recital for the 'Great Performers' series at Lincoln Centre.

Our son Thelonius would have been born a few months later. Followed, after another couple of years, by our daughter Emily.

Yes, by our daughter Emily . . .

Wait a minute, though: I can hear her crying. I can hear her crying downstairs.

No, it isn't her. It isn't Emily. It's the squeal of those big garage doors at the Watson Storage and Removal Company. Those rusty hinges. The first of the trucks has just arrived.

Do you want to know what I did say to her, instead? Do you want to know how I actually answered that question?

'Sure,' I said. 'There's an excellent B & B near here. Just around the corner. Halliwell's, on Bedford Street. It's just five minutes' walk.' And I looked away, to avoid glimpsing the disappointment that I knew would flare in her eyes, and I played the same two chords again, over and over, and I heard her thank me, and I kept on playing them, and she left, and I played them again, and two days later I went to Halliwell's to look for her, but they didn't know who I meant, and I said her name was Rachel but of course it wasn't, I made that up, I never knew her name, and I carried on playing those two chords and I'm still playing them now, this very moment, 9th and 13th, 9th and 13th, the sound of endless, infinite, unresolved possibilities. The most tantalizing sound in the world.

I don't know what chord I should play next. I can't decide.

V.O.

There came a point when it stopped being an interview and turned into a conversation. And there came another point, some time later, when it stopped being a conversation and turned into a flirtation. William could not have said when either of these things happened, with any certainty.

He did notice, however, that Pascale had laid aside her notebook, and was no longer writing down everything he said. And he noticed that they were no longer talking about his forthcoming film project, or his last CD, but had begun to discuss the unsatisfactory progress of her own career in journalism.

'Even now,' she was saying, 'I can't be sure that they will publish this article. And you know, that's annoying for you – because you have taken the trouble to talk to me – but also for myself, because it's a lot of work, to transcribe all of this and to write it up and then to be told that they don't want to use it after all.'

William smiled the self-deprecating smile at which he was so practised, and said: 'You make me wish that I was more famous. I'm sure if you were interviewing Jerry Goldsmith, or Michael Nyman . . .'

'No, not at all,' said Pascale. 'I can assure you that your film scores are very well known in France. They are very popular. It's just that – I don't know . . .' She shook her head, and stared ruefully into space. 'They are so unreliable, these people. They say one thing and they mean another.'

'I'd enjoy talking to you,' said William, after a pause, 'whether you were going to write about me or not.'

Pascale turned. For a moment he was convinced that the remark had sounded too crass, too forward. Her eyes were screened: all he could see in her Ray-Bans, dimly, was his own reflection. But the smile that now flickered onto her face was pleased rather than mocking.

Instead of responding directly to the compliment, she said: 'Are you enjoying the festival, so far?'

'Yes,' said William. 'Yes, I am.'

'It's not exactly Cannes. Not many celebrities, not many famous names.'

'Well, there's Claudia Remotti: wouldn't you say that she's one of Italy's biggest movie stars, these days? It's not often I get to spend so much time with a woman like that.'

Pascale pouted. 'So the jury spend a lot of time to-gether?'

'Absolutely. We watch the films together, we eat together, drink together . . .' But William was irritated, even as he said this, by the thought that he didn't know where the other jury members were at that moment. Were they socializing, somewhere, without having invited him – with-out even noticing that he wasn't there? Was some other man – that self-assured Spanish director, perhaps – sitting next to Claudia and plying her with alcohol? He felt a bitter pang of jealousy and poured more beer into Pascale's glass.

They were drinking at a seafront bar on a small promon-tory which jutted out from the shore, so that the ocean glimmered, turquoise and opalescent, on three sides. William's eyes were smarting from the white sunlight. He had forgotten to bring his sunglasses to France; had been on his way to buy some, in fact, when he had stopped at the bar for a drink and been waylaid by this charming jour-nalist. She had asked him if they could meet for a short interview some time during the week, and he had said that now was as good a time as any. It meant, admittedly, that he'd been unable to call his wife Alice at the time they had arranged – between two and three p.m. – but that was a small matter. She was bound to understand that an interview request should take precedence . . .

'I'm sorry?' he said now, conscious that he had not been listening to Pascale as she addressed a direct question to him.

'I said, Are you a fan of this kind of film? Horror films. Fantasy films. I wondered if you felt an affinity with this particular genre.'

William considered his answer carefully. His concern, as always, was not to express any firmly held opinion of his own, but to make sure that he did not give offence, or provoke disagreement: and since he had not yet learned Pascale's views on the subject, this was difficult.

'I think that serious artistic statements,' he said, pompously, 'can be made within any kind of generic restrictions. It doesn't do to be snobbish about these things. Horror films don't tend to be taken seriously by critics but if you look at many of the entries at this festival, you'll find that they are very finely crafted works of art – the works of real *auteurs*, real visionaries.'

'I'm sure you're right,' said Pascale, smiling at him with a furrowed intensity he already found endearing. 'And what film do you have to see this afternoon?'

William consulted his festival programme. '*Mutant Autopsy 3*,' he said, and signalled to the waiter for the bill.

The 14th Annual Festival of Horror and Fantasy Cinema was based in a large, modern, impersonal hotel about two kilometres from the centre of town. Although it housed a massive cinema auditorium, which would often be filled to capacity even for the most unpromising-sounding films, William soon realized that the hub of the festival was not here but in the bar on the ground floor. This bar was open to members of the public, as well as to the film-makers and critics, so there was always a fair smattering of Goths, slasher fans and gorehounds spread around the tables in a sea of black clothing and grey, bloodless complexions. But mainly it was a place where the festival insiders could exchange gossip and do deals. William soon got into the habit of going down there every evening at around 7.30, in the hope of seeing Claudia Remotti for a drink before dinner.

On the fourth night of the festival, just before leaving his room on this errand, William sat on his balcony and flicked idly through the programme to see what delights awaited the jury members during the rest of the week. He was getting tired of rapes, mutilations, ritual slayings, decapitations and chainsaw massacres. Apart from anything else, as the only composer on the jury he was supposed to be looking out for a potential winner of the best soundtrack award, and had been finding it hard to concentrate on the music that tended to accompany such scenes. He was ready, now, to see something a little more original, a little more sophisticated.

He held out little hope for tomorrow's offering, a Spanish movie billed as a 'hilarious necrophiliac comedy' called *One Corpse at a Time, Please!*; nor for the American film they would be seeing the day after that, *Vampire Brainsuckers Get Naked*. The last entry in the festival, however, looked marginally more interesting. It was a German film, a supernatural love story involving ghosts and out-of-body experiences, whose title translated as *The Haunted Heart*. He looked down the credits to see who had written the music, and found a name that he didn't recognize. Then he looked at the other credits and suddenly saw, in a spasm of wild astonishment, a name that he knew only too well.

Gertrud. Gertrud Keller. It was her screenplay. *She* had written this film.

William laid the programme aside, not quite sure how to digest this information. Well, she had made it, anyway – she had written something for the movies, just as she always said that she would. That was a cheering thought, wasn't it?

He realized at once that he needed a drink.

Fortune favoured him, on this occasion, and upon entering the bar the first person he saw was Claudia Remotti, sitting at a corner table and sipping champagne, with no more serious rival for his attentions than Michel, the festival administrator. Michel was a small, dapper man, his hair slicked neatly into place, his body giving off a permanent and overpowering aroma of sweet cologne. He was pleased to see William, having some important information to convey to all of the jury members.

'Tomorrow's film is from Spain,' he said, 'and as you will be aware from the programme, it is being shown in its V.O. format, or "Version Originale". This means that the print will be in the Spanish language, with French subtitles. So, naturally, we have had to make an arrangement for our non-French-speaking judges.'

This arrangement, it transpired, involved assigning to each of the judges their own personal translator, who would sit beside them in the dark and whisper a rough and ready English version of the French subtitles into their ears, while trying not to disturb the members of the paying public seated throughout the rest of the auditorium. It didn't sound the most satisfactory solution, and Claudia was, as usual, full of complaints as soon as Michel had left.

'Really,' she said, 'this festival is the most badly organized I have ever attended. I don't think I have ever been treated like this in my life. They put us up in this dreadful hotel, and make us watch these terrible movies all day. The food is shocking, quite shocking. And now they are even going to show us these crappy movies in a language we don't understand!'

William let her talk on, while his thoughts roamed elsewhere – heading back, against his will, to the news he had just learned from the festival programme, and all the painful recollections that came in its wake. Recently, he had given as little thought as possible to his trip to Berlin, four years ago, when he had been asked to write the incidental music for a new play by a then unknown dramatist called Gertrud Keller. Almost at once he had struck up an intense, intimate friendship with her, and it continued, by letter and phone, for several months after William's return to England. He had been so flattered by her attentions, his self-esteem so enhanced by the thought that this beautiful, stimulating and intelligent woman should take an interest in him, that he completely failed to see where the relationship was heading: failed to notice that he had allowed Gertrud – even encouraged her – to fall in love with him. By the time that he did notice, it was too late. Their final letters crossed in the post: his suggesting that they should break off contact, hers announcing that she had left her husband, Jakob, and was ready to start a new life with him in either Germany or England. William had not replied; and they had not seen, spoken or written to each other since.

But supposing – the possibility suddenly exploded in his mind, like a flash insert popping up on screen – supposing Gertrud was going to be attending the festival herself? It was normal for the stars, the director or other members of the production team to be invited when they had a film in competition. Had Michel asked her to come? William would have to find out, immediately. Michel had muttered something about going to the festival office. He would follow him there. There was no time to lose.

'William!' Claudia called after him, baffled, as he abandoned her in mid-flow, leaving his glass of champagne almost untouched. But he didn't seem to hear.

Michel proved elusive. William was unable to track him down until the next morning, when they met in the lobby of the hotel shortly before the screening of *One Corpse at a Time, Please!* Michel was at pains to assure him – rather impatiently – that Gertrud Keller would not be attending the festival, and swiftly moved on to the more pressing business of introducing him to Henri – the man who would be working as his personal translator.

'Pleased to meet you,' said William.

'What ho, old chap,' said Henri. 'Ripping weather we're having today, what?'

Henri, it seemed, was a local translator who was busily engaged upon an as yet unpublished French edition of the complete works of P. G. Wodehouse. While everyone else at the festival sported shorts, plimsolls and T-shirts, he was wearing a three-piece, double-breasted tweed suit and was smoking a shockingly pungent meerschaum pipe. He shook William warmly by the hand and said, 'Tell me, old bean, what news from Blighty?', in an accent that would once have guaranteed him a lifetime's employment on the BBC Home Service.

Today's film turned out to be a black comedy in the amoral, nihilistic mould popularized by Quentin Tarantino and his followers, and concerned a gang of necrophiliac bank robbers with a penchant not simply for killing their victims but for having sex with them afterwards. Most of the dialogue was not really germane to the plot at all, but consisted of cynical wisecracks which the characters would trade while indulging absentmindedly in the most grotesque and appalling acts of violence. During an early scene, for instance, there was an argument over the distribution of some loot, prompting one of the crooks to shove a pistol into his colleague's mouth and snarl a few words in rasping Spanish. William could catch little of what he was saying even from the French subtitles, and it was left to Henri to furnish him with an adequate translation.

'The gentleman with the scar,' he explained, in his plummy English drawl, 'says, "Suck on this, you tight-arsed motherfucker." Then he adds, "I don't know how the fuck you got involved in this shit-brained scheme, but the closest you're ever going to get to that fucking money is when I shove it up your bony fucking arse."' He sighed at the infelicities of this version. 'I'm giving you the merest gist of it, I'm afraid. Do forgive me, old fellow. It's a jolly poor show on my part.'

As the week went by, William became more and more aware of the presence of Pascale. She had developed an unerring knack for turning up at his elbow when he was least expecting it: at the bar, at the hotel's buffet lunches, on his daily promenades through the town and along the seafront. She told him about a small, little-visited beach she had discovered, ten minutes' walk from the hotel along a rocky cliff path, and for the last three mornings they had gone there together for a swim before breakfast. He liked her, there was no denying that. He liked her solemn eyes and her almost comical earnestness; he liked (of course) the fact that she considered him famous, and was so clearly in awe of him; he liked her doleful eyebrows and thick black hair; and he liked her body, or what he had seen of it on their swimming trips. But it was an odd feature of their blossoming friendship that they talked so little about their lives back home. Once or twice Pascale would bring up the subject of her feckless boyfriend in Paris, who had been seeing her for more than five years but still refused to move into her apartment; yet William did not return these confidences. He never once mentioned Alice's name – or, for that matter, ever referred to himself in anything but the first person singular. After all, it would be a mistake to let himself get too close to Pascale; to offer her anything like the intimacy that had proved so disastrous when he had shared it with Gertrud Keller. That, at any rate, was how he justified his reticence to himself.

On Thursday night, the penultimate night of the festival, someone suggested dinner away from the hotel, at a small restaurant down by the marina, and William found himself joining a party which also included Henri, Pascale and Claudia Remotti. Claudia was accompanied, on this occasion, by Stephen Manners, the young American star of *Vampire Brainsuckers Get Naked* – a film which, earlier that day, had been greeted with a standing ovation by the largely teenage audience. Stephen was muscular and over-tanned, with a mane of shoulder-length blond hair which gave him something of the look of a high-class male stripper. Buoyed up by the success of his film, he proved to be noisy, cheerful company, and his exhilaration soon infected the other diners. But a slight pall was cast over the meal when Henri hastily excused himself, just before dessert, and disappeared off to the toilets clutching his stomach. He had been the only person to order *moules*, and when he returned to the table his face was pale and sweaty.

'Frightfully sorry,' he explained. 'This is a blasted nuisance, but I'm having a spot of gyp with the old tummy, wouldn't you know. I think I'd better be popping off to bed – best place for me, eh what? Toodle-pip, old beans.'

Not long after he'd gone, Stephen also looked at his watch and started to yawn ostentatiously.

'Press conference first thing in the morning,' he said. 'Perhaps I'd better be turning in.'

'Oh, is that the time?' said Claudia. 'I didn't realize it was so late already.'

It was half-past nine.

'I'll walk you back to the hotel if you like,' said Stephen.

'Thank you,' said Claudia; whereupon they both rose to their feet with startling abruptness, said a cursory 'Good night' and promptly set off together at a resolute pace, the white of his shirt and the cream of her dress finally blurring into one bobbing dot of light, far in the distance.

'Hmm,' said William, once they had gone.

'Not exactly subtle,' Pascale agreed.

William tried to meet her eyes for a few seconds, then looked away. He found their steadiness unnerving.

'And then there were two,' he murmured, half to himself.

The night was alive with a delicate soundtrack of creaks and tinkles from the huddle of yachts moored at the marina, while the ocean itself lapped gently at the seaboard only a few yards from their table. Otherwise, all was quiet.

'Perhaps we should be getting back as well,' said William. But Stephen and Claudia had left them with a full bottle of white wine, and they could not let it go to waste.

It was almost midnight when they returned to the hotel, and curious things appeared to have happened along the way. There must have come a point when they stopped walking separately, and linked arms, leaning heavily into each other. And there must have come another point, shortly afterwards, when it seemed like a good idea to kiss, open-mouthed and at some length, beneath the whispering leaves of a restless palm tree. Once again, William could not have said when either of these things happened, with any certainty.

His mind fuzzy with alcohol, he could scarcely remember how they skirted the hotel bar – still throbbing with activity at this hour – and rode up to the third floor together in the glass-bottomed lift. His next moment of clarity came inside his room, when he realized that he was sitting on the bed and Pascale was kneeling in front of him, between his legs, her body pressed tightly against his. She had taken off her blouse and was naked from the waist up.

'I'm glad,' she was saying. 'I'm glad we decided not to do it that way.'

William frowned, even as he caressed the smoothness of her back.

'What way?'

'Like Stephen and Claudia. Going to bed together the moment they met. This way is better.' She kissed him tenderly. 'I can't separate sex from emotion. Can you?'

'You mean' – he drew away from her, very slightly – 'you mean that you have to be in love with someone, before you can sleep with them?'

'Maybe not in love . . .' She kissed him again, and reached her hands beneath his T-shirt. 'But there has to be trust. Don't you agree?'

Panic – a sudden sense of dread – began to seize him.

'Pascale, have you –?' He took hold of her arms and stilled their motion. 'Why . . . Why haven't you asked anything about me, all week? About my . . . home life?'

She looked at him gravely now, confusion in her eyes.

'Because – well, because from the way you've been behaving, it's obvious that . . . there's nothing to say.'

The silence between them, at this point, seemed endless, and immense.

'I'm right, aren't I?' Pascale said at last, louder now, and with a catch in her voice.

'I'm married,' William told her. 'I'm married and I have a child.'

He buried his face in his hands, partly out of remorse, partly to shield her now shameful nudity from his gaze. He sat there for a minute or more, not moving, not saying anything; and in that time, he heard her slip on her clothes, and go.

As it turned out, he did not have to wait long before seeing Pascale again. At the entrance to the cinema the next morning Michel was looking out for him, and Pascale was standing by his side. They both welcomed him with a smile: hers enigmatic, his pleased and self-congratulatory.

'We had quite a little crisis this morning,' Michel explained, 'when your translator phoned to say that he was sick in bed with food poisoning, and would not be able to attend the screening of today's film. But as it turns out, this delightful young lady – who tells me that you are already well acquainted – has kindly volunteered to step into the breach.'

'That's very good of her,' said William, and shook the hand which Pascale, rather dumbfoundingly, held out to him.

They took their seats together in the half-empty auditorium: it seemed that if anything could keep the festival's horror enthusiasts at bay, it was the prospect of a romantic German ghost story, shown in its original language, shot partly in black-and-white and targeted firmly at an art-house audience. William was disappointed, and hoped that this didn't provide an omen for the commercial fortunes of Gertrud's first venture into the cinema.

Then the lights went down, and the film began.

The following ninety minutes were among the strangest and most disconcerting of William's life.

The Haunted Heart told the story of a love triangle. The story of a married couple – both working in the theatre – who enjoy a quarrelsome but stable home life, until one day, a young painter encounters the woman in a café, and becomes her lover. Their affair, which consumes the woman entirely, only comes to an end when the painter dies in a boating accident while on holiday with his own wife and daughter. After a period of intense, almost unbearable mourning, the woman returns to her forgiving husband; and finally, having lived through months of terrible distress, she discovers that she is, at heart, relieved that her lover is gone. The affair had brought much unhappiness in its wake, and she now realizes that she is married to a kind and understanding man. All is well, until one day the painter's ghost appears at her home, and she sees that even now, the relationship is not quite over . . .

In many ways it was a clumsy and humourless film, and most of the audience were unimpressed. Often they would laugh at scenes which were meant to be taken seriously. But William was blind to both its merits and its defects. A myriad of tiny details – from the exterior shots of the Berlin theatre to the private language of jokes and catch-phrases which the lovers invented for themselves – instantly stirred up his memories of Gertrud. Every aspect of the film seemed to hold some special significance for him. Even the musical score (which would eventually, at his instigation, win the best soundtrack award) had sprung from their shared vocabulary, being based upon themes by Francis Poulenc – mainly the Clarinet Sonata, a recording of which he had once sent her as a gift. William sat through the film in a kind of trance, numb with shock. He would not have believed that any film, any narrative, any work of art, could have transported him so suddenly and irresistibly into the past.

But that was not all. This film may have reawakened him to the past, but it also never allowed him to forget the present. It never allowed him to forget for a moment that Pascale was sitting beside him, closer than ever before but at the same time more distant, with a new tone in her voice and a new meaning in her actions: teasing, now, and reproachful. She faithfully translated every word of the subtitles. All the endearments he had once exchanged with Gertrud were now replayed, and given back to him. All the messages she had encoded for him in this film now reached him through Pascale's voice. There were a number of sex scenes, and here it seemed that Pascale took an even greater satisfaction in the fullness and literalism of her translation. She repeated every word, every gasp, every broken phrase, her lips almost brushing against his ear but then pulling back, in a mocking parody of physical contact. She leaned into him, her leg against his thigh. He could feel the rise and fall of her breathing. He could smell her body in the pressing heat of the auditorium.

In the very last scene of the film, he could no longer be sure whether it was Gertrud or Pascale that was speaking to him.

Du hast mir nichts zu bieten, said the woman to her ghostly lover. *Das sehe ich nun. Es wäre freundlicher, wenn du mich in Ruhe ließt.*

The French subtitles said: *Tu n'as rien à m'offrir. Je peux le voir maintenant. Ce serait plus gentil de me laisser seule.*

And Pascale whispered in his ear: 'You have nothing to offer me. I see that now. It would be kinder if you left me alone.'

Für dich ist vorsichtiges Benehmen zugleich ein Freundliches. Du glaubst, daß du dich harmlos benimmst. Aber, meiner Meinung nach, bist du ein gefährlicher Mensch.

Pour toi, être prudent et être bon, c'est la même chose. Tu crois que ce que tu fais ne porte pas à conséquence. Mais je crois que tu es dangereux.

'You believe that by being cautious, you are being kind. You believe that what you do is safe. But I think you are a dangerous person.'

Damals hast du mir beinahe das Herz gebrochen.

Tu as failli me briser le coeur.

'You came close to breaking my heart.'

Bitte, kehr in deine Heimat zurück. Dort wirst du glücklicher sein. Manfred, kehr zurück.

S'il te plaît, retournes d'ou tu viens. Tu y seras plus heureux. Retournes-y, Manfred.

'Please go back to where you belong. You will be happier there. Go back, William.'

He turned towards her abruptly, and said: 'The character's name is Manfred, isn't it?' But Pascale did not answer. All he could see were her eyes, shining in the dark.

William sat alone in the cinema for some time after the audience had left. He could not collect himself, or will himself into motion. When he was at last able to leave, he drifted around the hotel in a daze, not noticing the people around him, not responding when they spoke to him.

He felt better after some lunch and a siesta. In the middle of the afternoon he went down to the reception desk and asked if he could leave a note for Pascale. He was told that she had checked out shortly after one o'clock. After that he could think of nothing else to do but walk into town, to look once again for the sunglasses he had been meaning to buy all week.

Diary of an Obsession

'To Sherlock Holmes she is always *the* woman.'

Sir Arthur Conan Doyle, *A Scandal in Bohemia*

1972

A boy of eleven, on holiday with his family on the Cornish coast, stops to look at the paperbacks in a seafront shop. A title catches his eye: *The Private Life of Sherlock Holmes*. The book has a lurid cover, on which Holmes's deerstalker frames the image of a half-naked woman. The boy is horrified. A young moralist, puritanical beyond his years, he worships the Sherlock Holmes stories and is appalled at what he assumes to be an act of desecration. Some cheap exploitation merchant, it seems, has taken the great detective and written a book of sleazy erotic adventures about him. The young boy shakes his head, saddened by the ways of the world.

1975

A Sunday night, full of horrors: school, tomorrow, and only the prospect of a night's television to keep it at bay. There is a film showing on BBC 1 tonight: *The Private Life of Sherlock Holmes*. I remember, dimly, seeing the novelization of the screenplay on my Cornish holiday some years ago, and being repelled by it. But the newspaper gives this film serious attention. The director, Billy Wilder, is apparently famous. I will watch the film.

Afterwards, I discuss it with my grandfather. It was he who introduced me to Sherlock Holmes in the first place. We share a passion for these stories, and a kind of mania for authenticity when it comes to their screen adaptations. He was not impressed: thought that Colin Blakely, as Dr Watson, was too vocal and strident. I can see his point. Robert Stephens, as Holmes, was not quite right either: there was a high-pitched campness to his performance that seemed almost absurd. And yet already something about this film haunts me. Something about the bachelor snugness of Holmes's apartment (sets designed by Alexander Trauner), about the melancholy of the Scottish countryside (photographed by Christopher Challis), which I can't get out of my head. Perhaps it's the music. A recurring motif is the famous theme from *Swan Lake,* and I find myself whistling it on the way to school the next morning.

1976

Somewhere, at the back of a novel (I have long forgotten the title), I find a list of other books available from the same publisher. One of them is the novelization of *The Private Life of Sherlock Holmes*. I order it, somehow not believing that it will ever arrive. But a few days later, a package appears for me in the post.

At this time, of course, it is not possible to 'own' films on video. You cannot see them whenever you want, or rewind and freeze-frame your favourite scenes. It is rare for original screenplays to be published, and so the existing technology really allows only one way of capturing and reliving your favourite movies: the novelization, that bastard, misshapen offspring of the cinema and the written word. At home, my bookshelves groan under the weight of these execrably written texts: cheap, hastily assembled adaptations of recent movies and TV series. And despite my feelings about Billy Wilder's film, I expect this one to be no better.

But I'm wrong. It's a beautifully judged pastiche of the Conan Doyle style, by two well-known writers, Michael and Mollie Hardwick. I enjoy it every bit as much as the original Holmes stories, and read it again and again, even when I should be reading my Shakespeare plays and my Jane Austen novels and all the other sacred cows of the British school system.

1978

A couple of years later, the film is on television again, and I realize that yes, the music is the key to its magic. But most of it is not by Tchaikowsky. It's by someone I have never heard of, until now: Miklós Rózsa. An adaptation of his own violin concerto, according to the opening credits. There is an aching, desperate sadness and *nostalgie* to the love theme in this movie, which seems – theoretically – to be at odds with the light-heartedness and brittle humour which characterizes the first hour or so. The combination shouldn't work, but it does.

There are two stories in the film: a mad Russian ballerina asks Holmes to become the father of her child, and he gets out of it by pretending that he and Dr Watson are homosexual. Then, a beautiful woman arrives at 221B Baker Street late one night, having apparently survived a murder attempt. She, Holmes and Watson go to Scotland together, to find her missing husband. During the course of their investigation, Holmes falls in love with her, but he discovers, in the end, that she is a German spy, and has been deceiving him all along. Months later, in the closing moments of the film, he learns that she has been executed by firing squad, and is heartbroken.

On this viewing, I notice that there is something odd about the movie. The shape of it is all wrong. The two stories – one lasting half an hour, the other lasting ninety minutes – don't seem to fit together. The pace is leisurely, but every so often there are sudden, unaccountable cuts from one scene to another. And some of the scenes which I enjoyed in the novelization – a diatribe from Holmes about ballet, delivered while sitting in the bathtub, and a long, present-day prologue in which Dr Watson's grandson arrives at a bank in modern London to retrieve his ancestor's lost manuscript – don't actually seem to be in the film.

And yet in spite of these odd, dislocating omissions, it seems to move me more deeply, and speak to me more directly, than any other film I have seen; and provokes me into a kind of frenzy of research and information-gathering.

Who is Miklós Rózsa?

In a tiny, Dickensian back street of Birmingham, Needless Alley, there is a record shop called Vincent's. At this point in my life (I am seventeen years old), I visit it all the time: at least two or three times a week. The proprietor, a tactiturn but well-informed man, has never heard of Miklós Rózsa. He looks him up in the catalogue, and orders for me an LP called *Rózsa Conducts Rózsa*. When it arrives in a couple of weeks, I discover that it is an album of film music, which contains pieces from Wilder's *Five Graves to Cairo*, Korda's *Lydia* and many other movies. There is also a ten-minute suite from *The Private Life of Sherlock Holmes*. At last, I can listen to that love theme whenever I want! But even this is not enough. I have a fetish for completeness. I need to hear the concerto from which it came. And there the owner of the shop cannot help me. There is one recording – made by Heifetz for RCA in the 1950s – but it has been out of print for years.

Next, I discover a book by Maurice Zolotow, called *Billy Wilder in Hollywood*. An odd sort of biography, composed of one part psychoanalysis and two parts salacious gossip. But it tells me some important things about the Sherlock Holmes film. The version released in the cinemas, the version I have seen on television, is only two-thirds of the completed film. Two whole stories, and numerous important scenes, were chopped out by Wilder at the studio's insistence. A flashback to Holmes's student days at Oxford, when the discovery that his girlfriend is really a prostitute confirms his lifelong misogyny. More details about his drug addiction, which gets so out of control that Dr Watson himself devises a phoney case about a corpse in an upside-down room, purely to get his friend away from the cocaine. Many others, as well. This was to have been Wilder's longest, most complex, most personal film. Now, all that remains are its ruins.

I know that I cannot rest until I have seen the original version.

1979

The British musicologist Christopher Palmer has written a monograph about Miklós Rózsa, which I have bought in London. The front cover is illustrated with some record sleeves, including the long-deleted RCA recording of his violin concerto. The reproduction is so clear that I can even read the catalogue number: LSC-2767. I travel to America for three months with my girlfriend, in the year before we go to university, and for some reason I am convinced that I will find this record there. I spend many hours one day in a gigantic record shop in Washington, thumbing my way through sleeve after sleeve: they seem to have every single recording from this series, except the one that I want. The frustration is unbearable.

The 1980s

I find a shop in London which sells film posters. I buy the poster for the film and hang it, successively, on the walls of each of the rooms I inhabit as a student at Cambridge and Warwick universities. It watches over me like a friendly muse as I secretly work on my first novels. And when the film is next shown on television, I have a brilliant idea: I connect my tape deck to the earphone socket on the television, and record the complete soundtrack. I lie awake at night, listening to the dialogue on my Walkman in the dark, until I know every line, every intonation off by heart.

But all traces of the original version seem to be lost. The National Film Theatre, staging a Wilder retrospective, cannot find a complete print of *The Private Life of Sherlock Holmes*. Other restorations come and go: Cukor's *A Star is Born* and Kubrick's *Spartacus*. Hitchcock's *Rear Window* and *Vertigo*, unseen for many years, are rediscovered and shown again. I hear of sporadic attempts to find the lost scenes from Wilder's movie, but no one succeeds.

As a postgraduate at Warwick University, I haunt the university library in search of tatters and fragments from the lost scenes. I comb through the back issues of film magazines. There is nothing in *Cahiers du cinéma* – I have the sense that they look down on Wilder, despise him for his literariness – but I find a long article in *Positif*, which contains a still from one of the missing sequences: Holmes contemplating a corpse in a room which has been turned completely upside-down, with the bed hanging from the ceiling and the lamp protruding from the floor. I photo-copy the image and store it in my files, like a child hiding some secret toy which he values too highly to share with the rest of the world.

1994

As I grow older, history begins to repeat itself, patterns begin to emerge. Today, there is another chance sighting on a bookstall: this time at Liverpool Street Station in London. Both in its themes and in the story of its fate at the hands of the studios, this film has become, for me, intimately bound up with ideas of loss: lost time, lost opportunities, the rapidity with which events recede into the past and can never be recaptured. And so it seems appropriate that this new discovery should occur on a day when I am travelling to Norwich, to reacquaint myself with an old schoolfriend whom I haven't seen for many years. Looking for a magazine to while away the two-hour train journey, I glimpse, incredibly, exactly the image which arrested my attention in Cornwall more than twenty years ago: the familiar outline of Holmes's deerstalker framing the image of a half-naked woman. But what magazine would conceivably want to put this picture on its cover?

A doomed magazine, certainly. Its name is *Movie Collector*, and it is fated only to last for a handful of issues. It caters to a small audience of fanatics, fetishists, obses-sives: people like myself, in short. It carries letters and art-icles about deleted footage, missing scenes, tiny shards of forgotten movies which have vanished into some kind of cinematic purgatory. And in the course of a long essay on *The Private Life of Sherlock Holmes* – containing information which is mainly, of course, known to me already – I learn this amazing news: that some of the lost material has been recovered, and is available in the form of an American Laserdisc.

Laserdiscs: the format is barely known to me, but within a few days I have become an expert. A mail-order company in England supplies me with a copy of the disc, which arrives in a gatefold sleeve like an LP from the 1970s, and I marvel at the shimmery, abstract beauty of this new technology. I can scarcely believe that this glittering object contains what it promises: two of the missing sequences, but in comically truncated form. One of them has video only (but lacks the soundtrack), the other has soundtrack only (but lacks the video). A black joke, in a way, almost worthy of Billy Wilder himself.

There is only one problem: I don't have a Laserdisc player.

The machines, apparently, cost £500: surely a small price to pay for something which will unlock parts of a mystery that has been plaguing me for two decades. But something holds me back. Can I justify this expense to my wife, at a time when we are struggling to buy furniture and re-decorate our flat? Suddenly this whole quest seems almost . . . frivolous. And there is another reason, somewhat harder to articulate. Part of me, I realize, would *prefer* this material to remain lost, unseen. That is its very essence. Take away that quality and you have destroyed something fragile, irreplaceable.

I will not play the disc, for the time being. It sits on a shelf, awaiting its moment: a shiny chalice of pure, unrealized potential.

1997

Technology changes everything, it seems. Suddenly everything has become more *retrievable*.

Music, for instance. Since the advent of the CD, there has been a vast expansion in the variety of classical music available to the consumer. Every conceivable byway of twentieth-century music can now be explored with a single visit to your local megastore. It can only be a matter of time before . . . And yes, sure enough, a recording of Miklós Rózsa's Violin Concerto appears, beautifully performed by Igor Gruppman and the New Zealand Symphony Orchestra. A small victory.

This music accompanies me in the months and years it takes me to complete a new novel, *The House of Sleep*. A novel about lost time, lost opportunities and so – naturally – lost movies. I invent a film reviewer called Terry whose absurd critical outpourings are a kind of punishment for all the journalistic crimes I myself have committed over the years. (He dismisses Wilder, quite wrongly, as a 'middlebrow talent'.) The novel contains only fleeting reference to *The Private Life of Sherlock Holmes*, but for those few people who love the film as I do, there is also a hidden network of codes and allusions: Ashdown, the name of my Gothic mansion, is also a name Holmes assumes in the film when he pretends to be a married man; Valladon, the name of the café where all the characters meet, is also the assumed name of the German spy with whom Holmes falls in love. And so on . . .

Meanwhile, I appear on a television programme to talk about Alfred Hitchcock's film *Sabotage*, and after the recording the producer tells me, in passing, that the BBC has facilities for viewing Laserdiscs, which I am free to use whenever I want. It seems almost ungracious to refuse this offer, so pressingly made. And so perhaps it is time to confront my demon after all.

I am accompanied that morning by my wife, who has lived with my obsession for years and watched it with the detached fascination of the former psychologist. We arrive at BBC Television Centre on an impossibly wet, cold, bleak weekday morning, and drink black coffee in the canteen before making our way to the screening room. The engineer takes the disc and I explain to him which sections I want to view. The lights go down a few minutes later, and the screen flickers into life.

It is important for some things to remain lost. A quality of evanescence is central to cinema. Despite the video revolution, a film should not be like a book, something to take down from the shelf and open whenever we want. You mustn't slip a copy of *Sansho the Bailiff* out of its case, and skim through a few minutes on your DVD player when you have a spare moment. It does violence to the medium. Cinema owners and TV schedulers are the real gods of film: a movie is something we should only see *when somebody else shows it to us*.

Of course I have a copy of *The Private Life of Sherlock Holmes* on video, but I don't watch it very often. I even have, on tape now, the audio and video versions of those missing scenes. But it comforts me to know that they are still incomplete, and that there remain other scenes from the film which are lost, perhaps irretrievably. This is how it should be. After all, I have not really been searching for the complete film all these years. I have been searching for something even more unreachable: trying to recapture, somehow, the sense of wonder, of security, of happiness I felt when I first saw the film on that Sunday evening, when it made me forget, for two blissful hours, my fear of returning to school the next day. It is that young self I have been trying to bring back to life. And perhaps my grandfather, too, who loved Sherlock Holmes almost as much as I did, and died fourteen years ago but has revisited my thoughts every day since.

The Private Life of Sherlock Holmes is maybe not a master-piece, in any of its versions. Do we even know what the masterpieces of cinema are any more? But to me, it is always *the* film.

Six months ago I was at a party and I mentioned its title to another guest – a young musician – who told me that his grandmother had worked on the novelization. Her name was Mollie Hardwick. I asked him if she would mind signing my copy and he said no, quite the opposite; she had been rather ill lately and to hear that somebody remembered her work would probably cheer her up. So I sent her my precious copy, and she signed it, in her frail, elderly hand, and returned it to me. It was the second time in my life that this book had arrived in the post. Events continue to repeat themselves, the circle reveals itself more and more clearly, but is never quite closed.

Postscript (2004)

Six years after writing this piece, I have little to add, except to mention two letters that it provoked. One – much to my surprise – was from the great Spanish novelist Javier Marias, who sent me a copy of the British edition of his novel *A Heart So White* inscribed 'To Jonathan Coe, with whom I think I share, at least, something mentioned on page 214'. He had read my article when it was published by *Cahiers du cinéma* as part of a series called '*Ecrire le cinéma*', and wanted me to know that he was haunted by the same film – and, in particular, by Miklós Rózsa's sound-track music.

Emboldened by this response, in part, I decided to write to Billy Wilder himself. I knew that he was in poor health (he was into his nineties), and I knew, too, from the biographies I had read, that he was still slightly bitter about the whole *Sherlock Holmes* experience: not just the mangling of the film at the hands of the executives, but also – and perhaps more keenly – its commercial failure in 1970. At the back of my mind, I suppose, was the rather morbid thought that he was going to die quite soon and I wanted him to know how much the film meant to me and many others.

I can't remember now what I said in the letter, except that I had also been authorized by the *Observer* to ask him for an interview. I enclosed a copy of my article and wrote to his home address, which I found on the internet in less than three minutes. Shortly afterwards, a letter arrived at my flat with a California postmark. He must have replied almost by return.

> *Dear Mr Coe,*
> *I am dictating this letter out of my sick bed. At 94 I have retired from Pictures and have not done one in twelve years.*
> *An interview with me would not be very rewarding. I am a little confused and not quite with it. But I do want to thank you for your piece in the French 'Ecrire le cinéma'.*
> *'Holmes' was not a success, it is wonderful to see that for somebody it has become an obsession.*
> *With warmest regards, I am yours,*
> *Billy Wilder*

POCKET PENGUINS

1. Lady Chatterley's Trial
2. **Eric Schlosser** Cogs in the Great Machine
3. **Nick Hornby** Otherwise Pandemonium
4. **Albert Camus** Summer in Algiers
5. **P. D. James** Innocent House
6. **Richard Dawkins** The View from Mount Improbable
7. **India Knight** On Shopping
8. **Marian Keyes** Nothing Bad Ever Happens in Tiffany's
9. **Jorge Luis Borges** The Mirror of Ink
10. **Roald Dahl** A Taste of the Unexpected
11. **Jonathan Safran Foer** The Unabridged Pocketbook of Lightning
12. **Homer** The Cave of the Cyclops
13. **Paul Theroux** Two Stars
14. **Elizabeth David** Of Pageants and Picnics
15. **Anaïs Nin** Artists and Models
16. **Antony Beevor** Christmas at Stalingrad
17. **Gustave Flaubert** The Desert and the Dancing Girls
18. **Anne Frank** The Secret Annexe
19. **James Kelman** Where I Was
20. **Hari Kunzru** Noise
21. **Simon Schama** The Bastille Falls
22. **William Trevor** The Dressmaker's Child
23. **George Orwell** In Defence of English Cooking
24. **Michael Moore** Idiot Nation
25. **Helen Dunmore** Rose, 1944
26. **J. K. Galbraith** The Economics of Innocent Fraud
27. **Gervase Phinn** The School Inspector Calls
28. **W. G. Sebald** Young Austerlitz
29. **Redmond O'Hanlon** Borneo and the Poet
30. **Ali Smith** Ali Smith's Supersonic 70s
31. **Sigmund Freud** Forgetting Things
32. **Simon Armitage** King Arthur in the East Riding
33. **Hunter S. Thompson** Happy Birthday, Jack Nicholson
34. **Vladimir Nabokov** Cloud, Castle, Lake
35. **Niall Ferguson** 1914: Why the World Went to War

POCKET PENGUINS

36. **Muriel Spark** The Snobs
37. **Steven Pinker** Hotheads
38. **Tony Harrison** Under the Clock
39. **John Updike** Three Trips
40. **Will Self** Design Faults in the Volvo 760 Turbo
41. **H. G. Wells** The Country of the Blind
42. **Noam Chomsky** Doctrines and Visions
43. **Jamie Oliver** Something for the Weekend
44. **Virginia Woolf** Street Haunting
45. **Zadie Smith** Martha and Hanwell
46. **John Mortimer** The Scales of Justice
47. **F. Scott Fitzgerald** The Diamond as Big as the Ritz
48. **Roger McGough** The State of Poetry
49. **Ian Kershaw** Death in the Bunker
50. **Gabriel García Márquez** Seventeen Poisoned Englishmen
51. **Steven Runciman** The Assault on Jerusalem
52. **Sue Townsend** The Queen in Hell Close
53. **Primo Levi** Iron Potassium Nickel
54. **Alistair Cooke** Letters from Four Seasons
55. **William Boyd** Protobiography
56. **Robert Graves** Caligula
57. **Melissa Bank** The Worst Thing a Suburban Girl Could Imagine
58. **Truman Capote** My Side of the Matter
59. **David Lodge** Scenes of Academic Life
60. **Anton Chekhov** The Kiss
61. **Claire Tomalin** Young Bysshe
62. **David Cannadine** The Aristocratic Adventurer
63. **P. G. Wodehouse** Jeeves and the Impending Doom
64. **Franz Kafka** The Great Wall of China
65. **Dave Eggers** Short Short Stories
66. **Evelyn Waugh** The Coronation of Haile Selassie
67. **Pat Barker** War Talk
68. **Jonathan Coe** 9th & 13th
69. **John Steinbeck** Murder
70. **Alain de Botton** On Seeing and Noticing